THE MIXED-UP MICE

BY ROBERT KRAUS

IN THE BIG BIRTHDAY MIX-UP.

WARNER
JUVENILE
BOOKS

A Warner Communications Company

New York

Suggested for readers ages 5 and up.

Warner Juvenile Books Edition
Copyright © 1990 by Robert Kraus
All rights reserved.
Warner Early Reader™ is a trademark of Warner Books, Inc.

Warner Books, Inc., 666 Fifth Avenue, New York, NY 10103
Ⓦ A Warner Communications Company

Printed in the United States of America
First Warner Juvenile Books Printing: August 1990
10 9 8 7 6 5 4 3 2 1

Library of Congress Cataloging-in-Publication Data

Kraus, Robert, date.
    The Mixed-Up Mice in the big birthday mix-up / by Robert
Kraus.—Warner Juvenile Books ed.
        p.   cm.
    For 5-8 year olds.
    Summary: The Mixed-Up Mice buy presents for each other
in the mistaken belief that one of them is having a birthday.
    ISBN 1-55782-338-3
    [1. Birthdays—Fiction.   2. Gifts—Fiction.   3. Mice—Fiction.]
I. Title.
PZ7.K868Mm   1990
[E]—dc20
                                        90–33050
                                            CIP
                                            AC

The Mixed-Up Mice know it's somebody's birthday!

Dad thinks it's Mom's birthday.

Mom thinks it's Dad's birthday.

Junior thinks it's Sis's birthday.

Sis thinks it's Junior's birthday.

Without telling each other, they buy presents for each other.

Can you find the Mixed-Up Mice at Mouse Mall?
Has a cat sneaked in?

Back home,
the Mice secretly
make birthday cakes

nd plan to surprise
he birthday person.

LATER THAT DAY . . .

"It's not my birthday," says Mom.

"It's not my birthday," says Dad.

Make way for Junior!

Here comes Sis!

The Mixed-Up Mice decide to exchange presents anyway.

The Mice all agree that presents are nice anytime.

But the big question still has not been answered.

It's George Washington's birthday!
And the Mixed-Up Mice didn't get him anything!

Sis and Junior
hurry to the store
to buy a birthday card
for George Washington.

Sis and Junior can't find a birthday card they like . . .

so they choose a get well card and go home
to show it to Mom and Dad.

The Mixed-Up Mice promise to talk about things from now on so there won't be any more mix-ups.

The Beginning.